BELLA'S BRAZILIAN FOOTBALL

IN & ELKE STEINER

MILET

Milet Publishing, LLC
333 North Michigan Avenue
Suite 530
Chicago, IL 60601
Email info@milet.com
Website www.milet.com

First published by Milet Publishing, LLC in 2007

Copyright © 2007 by Adam Guillain for text
Copyright © 2007 by Elke Steiner for illustrations
Copyright © 2007 by Milet Publishing, LLC

ISBN 978 1 84059 488 1

Printed in China

Please see our website www.milet.com for more
titles featuring Bella Balistica.

BELLA'S BRAZILIAN FOOTBALL

ADAM GUILLAIN & ELKE STEINER

"Football? It's the beautiful game." Pelé

From the slums of Três Corações in Brazil came the footballing
legend Edson Arantes do Nascimento – otherwise know as
Pelé, 'The King' of football.

Bella Balistica was born in Guatemala and now lives with Annie,
her adoptive mother, in London. She discovers a magical
pendant that had once belonged to her Guatemalan birthmother
and is instantly connected with her animal twin –
the resplendent Quetzal bird – and her adventures begin . . .

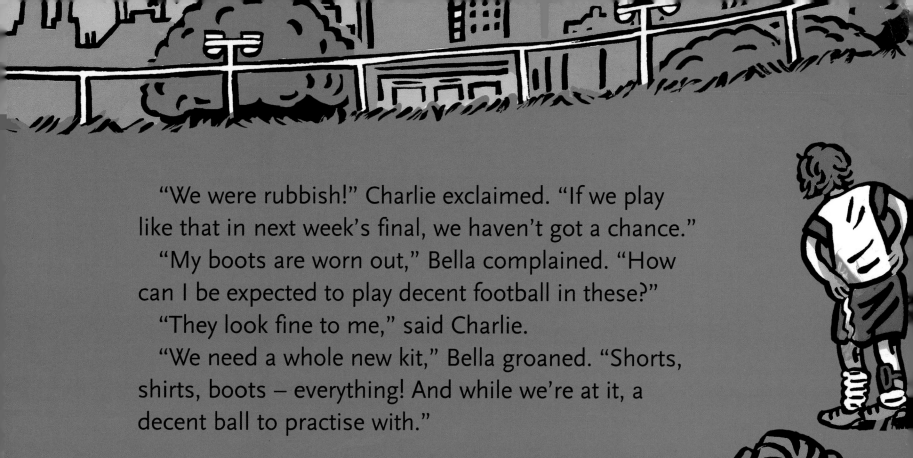

"We were rubbish!" Charlie exclaimed. "If we play like that in next week's final, we haven't got a chance."

"My boots are worn out," Bella complained. "How can I be expected to play decent football in these?"

"They look fine to me," said Charlie.

"We need a whole new kit," Bella groaned. "Shorts, shirts, boots – everything! And while we're at it, a decent ball to practise with."

As always, Bella's mother Annie was there to support her daughter.

"Bad luck, Bella. You played really well," she said, as she walked Bella towards the changing rooms.

"We lost 4–nil," said Bella, flatly. "We need some Brazilian football skills."

"Perhaps you just need to practise hard and work as a team," Annie suggested.

As soon as Bella got home, she changed into her favourite football shirt and trainers and stomped up to the attic.

She went to the old Guatemalan chest stuffed with her mum's amazing travel souvenirs and pulled out her jewellery box. Carefully unlocking its secret compartment, Bella took out the magical pendant that had once belonged to her Guatemalan birthmother. It was the pendant that gave Bella her powers and connected her with her animal twin.

The moment she slipped it on there was a sharp tapping at the skylight.

"You're not playing as a team," scolded the Quetzal when Bella opened the window to let him in.

"We need new boots and a new ball!" said Bella, defiantly.

"And some Brazilian football skills apparently," said the Quetzal, sarcastically. "Well, come on then."

"Where are we going?" Bella asked.

"Brazil, of course," said the Quetzal, turning to fly.

"Great," Bella exclaimed. "I'll bring the map."

Bella quickly rolled up her football map and flew through the skylight after the Quetzal. Below them, some of Bella's team-mates were playing football in the local park.

"We haven't even got a marked-out pitch to train on," Bella complained. "I bet it's not like that in Brazil."

"You're right there," said the Quetzal.

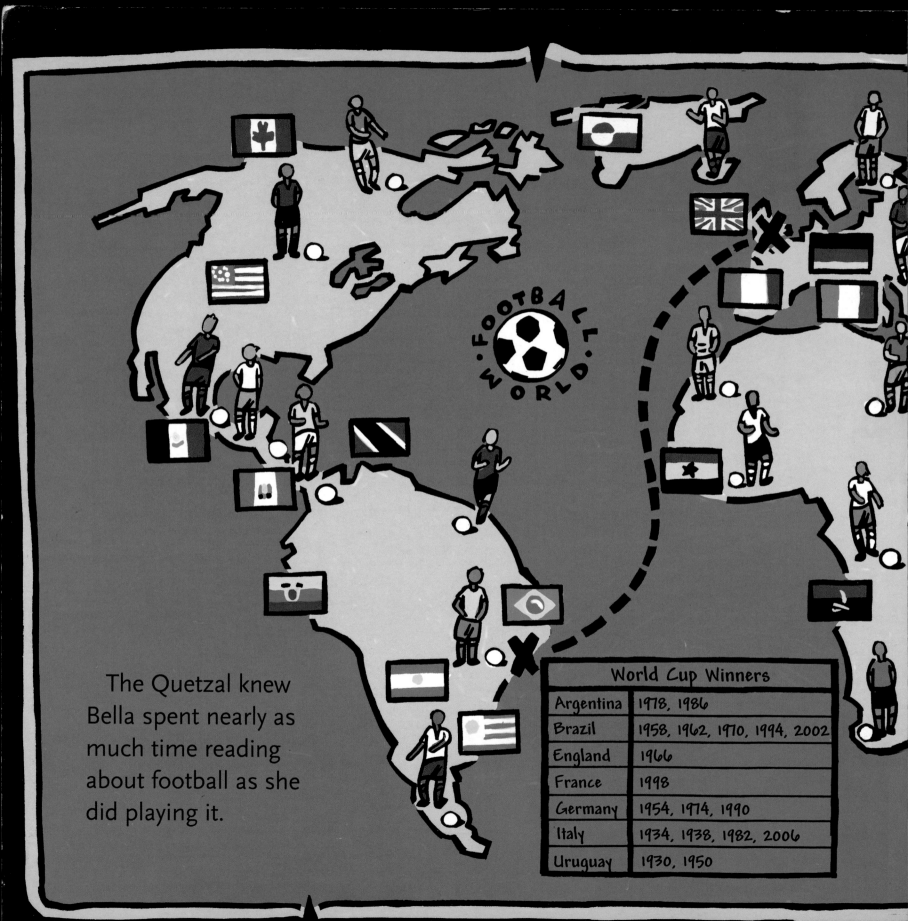

The Quetzal knew Bella spent nearly as much time reading about football as she did playing it.

World Cup Winners	
Argentina	1978, 1986
Brazil	1958, 1962, 1970, 1994, 2002
England	1966
France	1998
Germany	1954, 1974, 1990
Italy	1934, 1938, 1982, 2006
Uruguay	1930, 1950

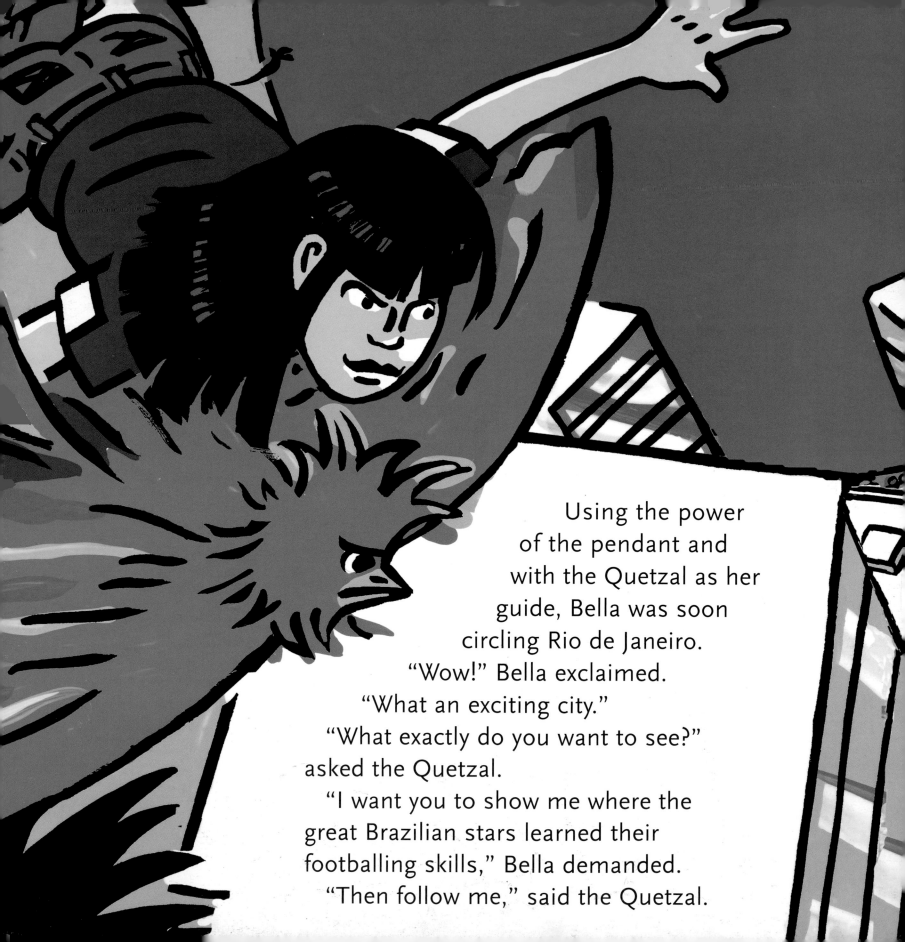

Using the power of the pendant and with the Quetzal as her guide, Bella was soon circling Rio de Janeiro.

"Wow!" Bella exclaimed. "What an exciting city."

"What exactly do you want to see?" asked the Quetzal.

"I want you to show me where the great Brazilian stars learned their footballing skills," Bella demanded.

"Then follow me," said the Quetzal.

Bella was expecting a glamorous football stadium. Instead she got to see a gang of street-children playing by a rubbish dump.

"I said I wanted you to show me where the great Brazilian stars learned their footballing skills," Bella moaned.

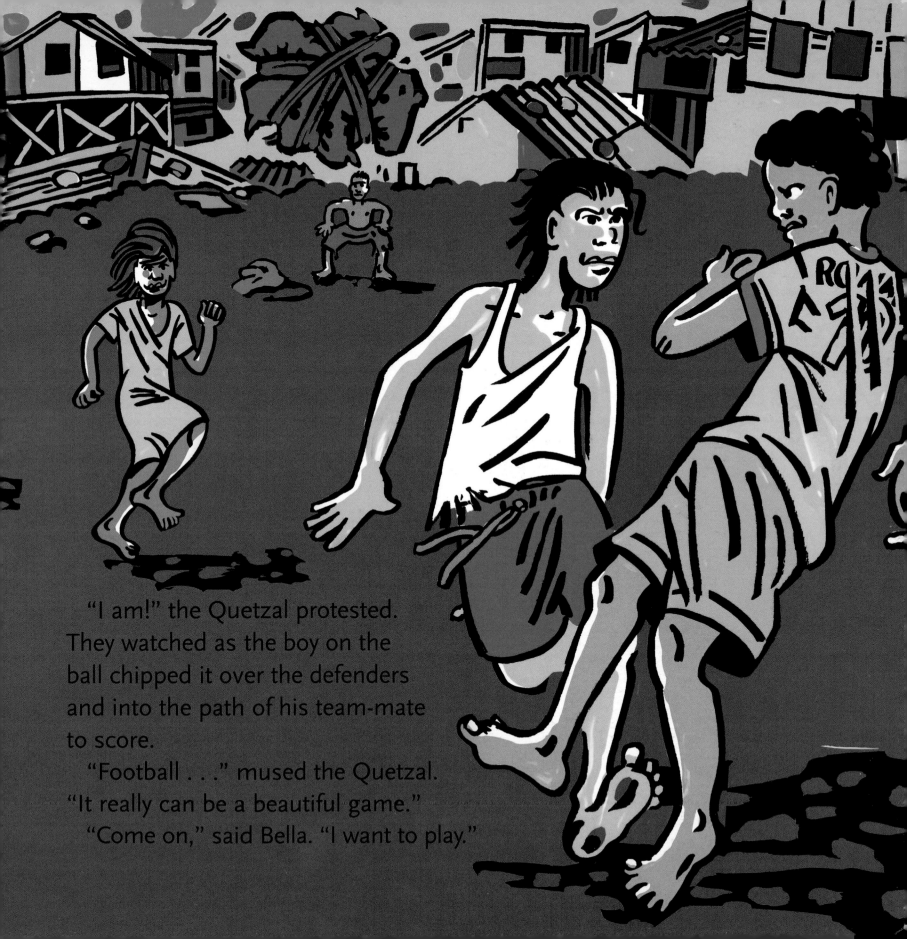

"I am!" the Quetzal protested. They watched as the boy on the ball chipped it over the defenders and into the path of his team-mate to score.

"Football . . ." mused the Quetzal. "It really can be a beautiful game."

"Come on," said Bella. "I want to play."

The other children looked at Bella's kit and trainers and were a little suspicious at first, but they still let her play.

"Stop passing the ball to where I am," complained the boy they called Ronaldo. "Imagine where I will be in five seconds and put it there."

Bella was impressed how everyone in her team kept moving, drawing defenders and opening up spaces for the strikers to run into. Thinking about what Ronaldo had told her, she passed the ball into a space just outside the box she hoped he could get to in time. He did – and he scored.

"That's better," Ronaldo cheered. "That's teamwork!"

After the match, Ronaldo and Bella got talking.
"Wouldn't you just love a new football and a decent pair of boots?" asked Bella.

"I would," smiled Ronaldo. "But most Brazilian footballers start out practising on the streets like this. It's not the boots and balls that make us play well. We've won the World Cup so many times because we know that no one player is greater than the whole team."

Ronaldo wanted
to show Bella his
Brazilian football cards.
He took her to the old
derelict bus many of the
children shared as their home.

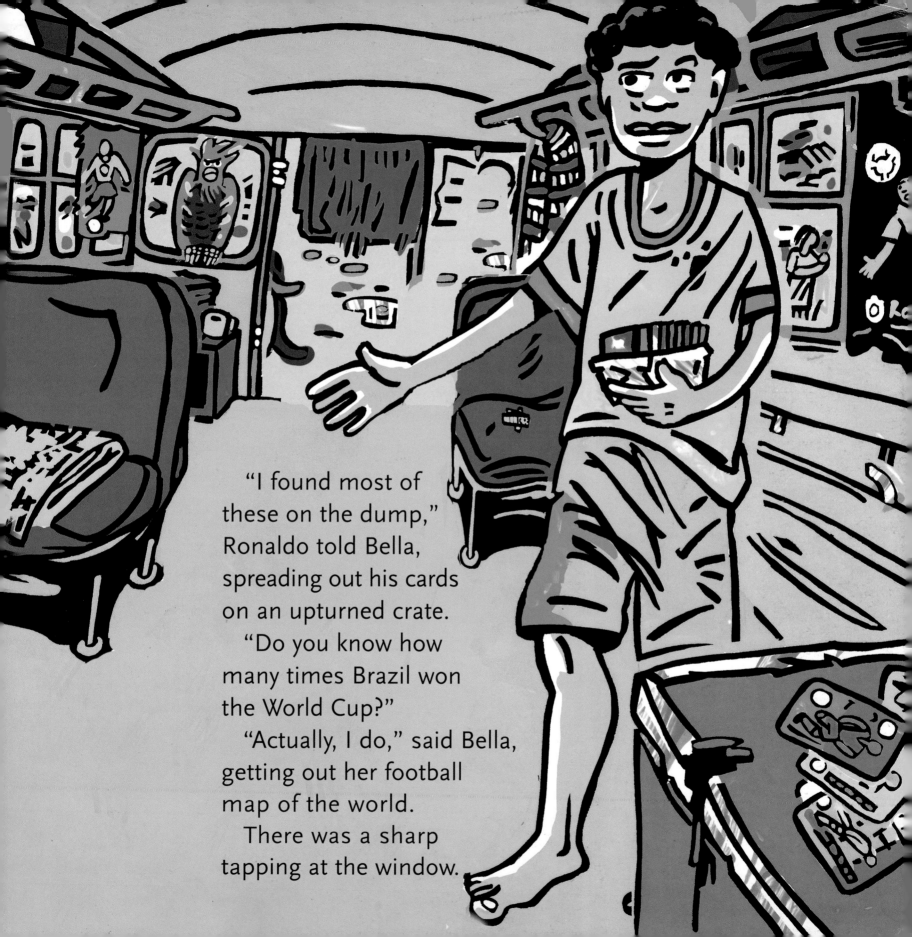

"I found most of these on the dump," Ronaldo told Bella, spreading out his cards on an upturned crate.

"Do you know how many times Brazil won the World Cup?"

"Actually, I do," said Bella, getting out her football map of the world.

There was a sharp tapping at the window.

"Hurry up," squawked the Quetzal. "It's time for your tea. I can play some tricks with time but I can't stop it forever."

"I've got to go," said Bella, sadly. "My mum's probably wondering where I am."

She rolled up her World Cup map and gave it to Ronaldo. "I want you to have this," she said. Ronaldo was delighted.

"And you must take this," he told Bella, handing her his ball.

"Thanks," smiled Bella, turning to leave. "And now I really must fly."

As they waved goodbye, both Bella and Ronaldo found it amazing to think they had so much in common with someone who lived so far away.

"What do you think about your chances for next week's final?" asked the Quetzal.

"We need to practise some new moves," said Bella. "But I have a few ideas."

At the final, no one could believe how well
Bella's school team played.

"They're passing the ball so well," Annie said to
Charlie's mother.

"And running so hard into the spaces," replied
Charlie's mum.

It was the pass that Bella and Charlie had been
practising all week that won the match.

"Looks like all that practice you did with your lucky ball really worked," smiled Annie. "How about we go shopping tomorrow and buy you a new pair of boots?"

"Thanks, mum," said Bella. "But these boots are fine for now."

"What about a new ball then?" asked Annie.

Bella took a long look at her Brazilian football and smiled.

"I like this one," she replied. "It's the best ball I've ever had!"